Babette Cole

PRINCESS SMARTYPANTS

AND THE FAIRY GEEK MOTHERS

Hodder Children's Books

HODDER CHILDREN'S BOOKS

First published in Great Britain in 2017 by Hodder and Stoughton

1 3 5 7 9 10 8 6 4 2

Text and illustrations copyright © Babette Cole 2017

The moral rights of the author have been asserted.

All characters and events in this publication, other than those clearly
in the public domain, are fictitious and any resemblance to
real persons, living or dead, is purely coincidental.

A CIP catalogue record for this book
is available from the British Library.

ISBN 9781-444-93160-0

Printed and bound by Clays Ltd, St Ives plc

The paper and board used in this book
are made from wood from responsible sources.

Hodder Children's Books
An imprint of
Hachette Children's Group
Part of Hodder and Stoughton
Carmelite House
50 Victoria Embankment
London EC4Y 0DZ

An Hachette UK Company
www.hachette.co.uk

www.hachettechildrens.co.uk
www.babette-cole.co.uk

Babette did not provide a dedication for this last book. So in place of her words, we would like to dedicate it to her – the uniquely talented creator who we were so very proud to publish.

CONTENTS

ᕤ INTRODUCTION ᕦ

Princess Smartypants is a very unusual, very modern princess.

Most princesses want to get married, but our princess prefers to run her kingdom without any princes messing things up.

This is not to say she does not get marriage proposals quite often. But any prince dumb enough to try to kiss our Princess Smartypants will be turned into a frog or slimy toad.

Princess Smartypants governs her wacky kingdom of Totaloonia very successfully. She does this with the help of her best friend and handyman giant, Eric the Annihilator, her court magician and super-geek, Mervin, and a castle full of unusual pets.

Having just rescued three
fairytale princes and seen
them happily married off to
her friends Cindy, Punzie and
Snowy, Princess Smartypants
and Eric were hoping for a bit
of peace and quiet from
sorting out problems.

However, just across the
ocean lies the kingdom of
Fairytale Land, which runs on
the usual fables, stories and
nursery rhymes most children
grow up with.

Doris, Smartypants' long-
lost fairy godmother, has just
arrived to tell her about the

trouble in Fairytale Land. All
the stories are going wrong!

Princess Smartypants
knows how important proper
fairytales are. Someone has to
keep them going or children
won't believe in magic and

happy endings, and they will
have nothing to dream about.

So straighten your tiaras, sit
comfortably and get ready for
Fairytale Land's most shocking
scandal yet!

CHAPTER 1

PLIGHT OF THE FAIRY GODMOTHERS

Princess Smartypants was gobsmacked when her long-lost fairy godmother, Doris Roundbotham, turned up at Castle Totaloonia with some very alarming news.

Doris sat on the sofa looking very bedraggled in her headscarf and crossover pinafore. A dusty-looking wand stuck out of her handbag. It was clear she was very upset.

'It's very bad news for fairytales and nursery rhymes,' she sighed. 'They're all going wrong.

All the endings have suddenly
changed. We fairy godmothers
can only grant three good
wishes at a time, but now
everyone is buying their
wishes from something called
www.wishit.com. Customers

can order as many as they like
and most people are choosing
bad ones! Thumbelina wished
she was a giant and is kicking
down castles all over the
place.'

Doris paused to slurp her tea and take a bite from a sparkly fairy cake.

'It's the most outrageous thing ever to happen to our kingdom,' she went on. 'We fairy godmothers have lost our jobs! And on top of that, if this doesn't stop soon, children will have no proper fairy stories to believe in. No magic, no happy endings and no dreams coming true. Everything we love about fairytales will be lost.'

Princess Smartypants and Eric looked at each other and

sighed. The last thing they needed was another irritating problem from Fairytale Land, but this one did sound particularly bad.

'I think we need the help of my court magician, Mervin,' Princess Smartypants said.

With a PING! Mervin appeared on the sofa next to Doris.

'Did someone call?' he asked.

Princess Smartypants and Doris explained the Fairytale Land catastrophe to Mervin. He started up his laptop and typed in www.wishit.com.

It was an online shop, as Doris had said. Just pay a fee and you could have any wish you liked!

'This is dangerous stuff!' Mervin exclaimed. 'Luckily, I've found the address for the office of wishit.com.'

It was:

Necromancy Nook,

Spellbound Path,

Fairytale Land.

'Oh NO!' Princess
Smartypants cried. 'That's
Araminta Allspell's house. We
should have known she'd be
involved in this trickery. She
may only look six years old
but she is really six hundred
and a very experienced witch
indeed.'

'She is also very greedy,'
added Mervin.

'What a nuisance. This
Aramita whatshername has
obviously found out she can
make loads of money by

magicking up any old wish she
likes, putting me out of work.
What can we do, Smartypants?
Are you willing to help me?'
Doris asked, dusting glitter
icing from her top lip.

'Of course, Fairy Godmother
Doris! You can count on me!'
Princess Smartypants said.

'But first things first. Let's go to Fairytale Land and see what damage has already been done.'

'Hmm,' said Eric. 'I don't like this one bit. It might be a trick to get us to leave Totaloonia so Araminta can cause trouble here again. I'll stay behind and guard the kingdom while you three investigate Fairytale Land.'

They all agreed this was a good idea. Princess Smartypants, Doris and Mervin climbed aboard Amazonia Sizzleflame, her best flying Crocodrag in Totaloonia, and

flew away to the far-flung
forests of Fairytale Land.

Far below in Necromancy Nook a good deal of plotting was going on.

CHAPTER 2

THE FAIRY
GEEK MOTHERS

Araminta Allspell was at home with her pet crow, Calliper, who was sitting on her shoulder and cackling away to himself.

Sitting around her table were three young girls dressed in silver and blue jumpsuits with lace-up knee boots and metallic capes. Their white permed hair looked as if it had been electrified. They wore earphones and stared deeply at their computer tablets.

Their names were Emily Encode, Harriet Hotkey and Gloria Gigabyte. They called

themselves 'The Fairy Geek
Mothers'. They had come
as part of the deal when
Araminta bought her new
techno smartphone from
Witchphone Warehouse.

The Geek Mothers were
watching the email orders for

wishes come rolling in to their inboxes.

'Here's a good one,' said Gloria Gigabyte. 'It's from some chick called Mary. She's wished for a black lamb so it will get lost at night and stop following her about.'

'I can conjure that up in seconds with a bit of poisonous mushroom and a bat wing, and it will cost her one thousand fairyflonks,' grinned Araminta.

'Maybe we should do a bit of advertising?' suggested Emily Encode. 'Have you ever wanted your magic mirror to tell your sister how ugly she is? Contact the Fairy Geek Mothers at wishit.com and your wish will come true.'

They all roared with laughter, but when Fairy Geek Mothers laugh it's more like a thunderclap, so the house shook a bit. Several bats fell off the wall and a teapot smashed.

'Get your princely brother a pair of our e-underpants and zap him on the bum with our mega-ray botty-blaster,' added Harriet Hotkey. There was more laughter, and Araminta's bottles of pickled slugs burst.

'Wish for a big hairy wart on the end of your least favourite princess's nose,' giggled Gloria Gigabyte, and the chandelier came crashing down on the table.

'Just think what mischief we can make!' gloated Araminta. 'We should definitely do some advertising.'

The Geek Mothers agreed and declared the meeting to be over. They turned back to their computers and started typing madly.

Meanwhile, Araminta couldn't resist tiptoeing down into her cellar to count the huge piles of treasure she'd collected so far by granting dodgy wishes. She danced around on top of a heap

of golden fairyflonk coins,
crowns, tiaras, sceptres,
precious jewels, golden plates
and silver goblets.

'Ha ha!' she cackled. 'No
one will know it's me behind
all this. They'll blame it
on the Fairy Geek Mothers
because they're in charge of
the website, wishit.com. I'm
as safe as a rat up a drainpipe,
Calliper.'

'Crawk!' said Calliper and
they rushed around the cellar,
shrieking grisly
laughs.

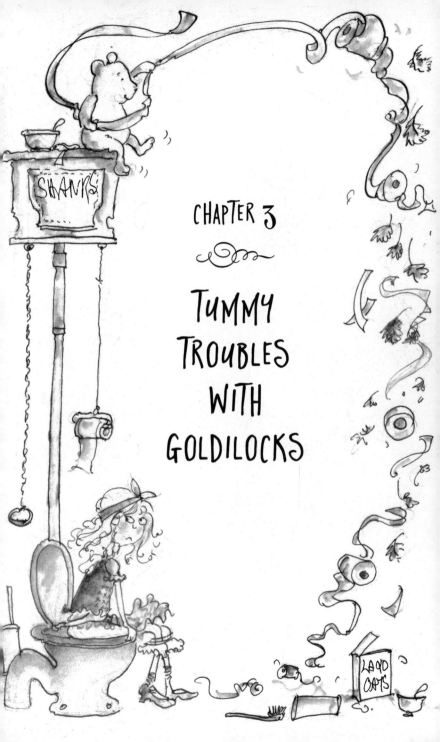

CHAPTER 3

TUMMY
TROUBLES
WITH
GOLDILOCKS

'We'd better check up on Goldilocks first. She's one of my regulars,' Doris said.

Amazonia Sizzleflame left Princess Smartypants, Doris and Mervin in a clearing near a small cottage.

'My goodness, the drains whiff a bit,' said Mervin, holding his nose as they approached the little house.

Doris knocked on the door.

'Just a minute,' a small voice called. There came the sound of a toilet flushing.

Eventually a little girl with curly golden hair opened the door and invited them inside.

'Hello Goldilocks,' said
Doris. 'This is my goddaughter
Princess Smartypants and her
court magician Mervin—'

But as soon as they sat
down, Goldilocks rushed
upstairs.

The flush sounded again.

'I really am sorry,' said the little girl when she came back. 'But my tummy has been so upset since my last visit to the bears' house. I know I need to visit them to keep the traditional fairytale working, but I'm not going any more because there's something wrong with their porridge.'

'Here,' Mervin said, conjuring up some bungup leaves. 'Chew one of these three times a day and you'll be as right as rain in no time.'

'Oh, thankyouvrrrymch,' Goldilocks replied through a mouthful of leaf.

After they'd left Goldilocks' cottage, Doris suggested they visit the Three Bears' house. It was just a short walk along the forest path.

Mummy Bear opened the door. She was pleased to see Doris and her friends.

'What have you done to Goldilocks?' asked Doris. 'She's not well at all and she thinks it's because of your porridge oats.'

'Well,' said Daddy Bear,

coming to the door. 'We got so fed up with her breaking in, scoffing our porridge, sleeping in our beds and leaving the place in a mess that we decided to do something about it. I found this website that could grant wishes, so we paid them all our savings and made a wish that she would stop being such a nuisance.'

'They charged us extra money for these Laxo Oats,' said Mummy Bear, holding up a packet. 'They said that after a bowl of these she would never return.'

'It worked,' said Daddy
Bear. 'She's not been back
since.'

'Yes, and nobody's been
sleeping in my bed,' squeaked
Baby Bear. 'Now it's too cold

for me to get into because nobody's warmed it up.'

Princess Smartypants and Doris explained that Goldilocks had a very poorly tummy because of their wish.

'Laxo Oats make you spend most of your time on the toilet!' exclaimed Doris.

The bears looked very sorry.

'We didn't know!' Mummy Bear said.

'You're all in a very important fairytale,' said Smartypants. 'And this is a bad ending for Goldilocks.'

The bears reluctantly agreed. The Laxo Oats were thrown in the bin and the story went back to normal without anyone knowing what had happened.

In the real fairytale, the bears are furious with Goldilocks for messing up their

house while they're away. But
now Goldilocks has arranged
to come back the next day and
clean up all the mess while the
bears go off to Center Parcs for
a Human Watch day out.

'Ooh!' said Smartypants, taking out her mobile phone. 'I've just got a text from Eric. He's been on the wishit website and they have loads of new reviews so business must be going well. We should go now.'

And with that Doris, Mervin and Princess Smartypants climbed aboard Amazonia and flew off to deal with the next fairytale disaster.

CHAPTER 4

THE GHASTLY GRANNIES

Amazonia flew over the trees until Doris spotted Red Riding Hood's granny's house. The Crocodrag landed gracefully, taking care not to bump into the tiny cottage.

Doris knocked on the door.

'Granny, is that you?' Little Red Riding Hood said, opening the door. She was wearing her beautiful red hoodie.

Doris introduced Princess Smartypants and Mervin to Red Riding Hood and explained about all the wishes going wrong.

'That's fantastic. Perhaps
you can help me find my
granny,' said the little girl.
'It's not like her to leave me at
home alone. She wrote me a
note.'

She handed over the piece
of paper to Doris.

Dear Granddaughter,

I'm fed up with waiting for your baskets of rock-hard cakes and fish-paste sandwiches so I bought a wish from wishit.com and checked into Elderly Gables five-star retirement home. It's lovely here and I'm being looked after very well. It has a swimming pool, a beauty salon, a spa and a top chef. They even do manicures. My nails are long and glittery red now. And I've had my teeth whitened.

All the better to eat you with.

    Love,

    Granny

'I don't like the sound of this "all the better" stuff,' said Princess Smartypants.

'Me neither. Maybe she's already been swallowed by the Big Bad Wolf, and he wrote the letter,' said Doris. 'Now he's off to Elderly Gables to gobble some more grannies!'

They all looked at each other in alarm before jumping on Amazonia's back and flying as fast as they could towards the retirement home.

They soon landed in the grounds of a very smart

country house with black
and white gables, several tall
towers and exactly thirty-six
peacocks in the garden.

'Can I help you?' asked
the receptionist. She had
remarkably long ears and
nails.

'We're looking for my grandmother, Granny Riding Hood,' said the little girl.

'Grrr,' said the receptionist, staring down her long nose and showing off some impressive teeth. 'She's on the lawn, about to have lunch with the other grannies.'

'I don't like the sound of that,' said Mervin.

'If we're not careful, WE could be lunch!' worried Red Riding Hood.

They made their way through the lavender plants and rose bushes in the garden until a large lawn spread out in front of them. Lots of wolf-like grannies were sitting in deckchairs waiting to be served lunch.

All of them looked exactly the same in dressing gowns, mob caps and glasses. They had long ears, bushy tails, big eyes and even bigger teeth.

'Which one's yours?' asked Princess Smartypants.

'There's no way of telling,' answered Red Riding Hood. 'She doesn't usually look like this. Hopefully she'll recognise me.'

'Oh, there you are, my dear,' said a big hairy granny sitting at a table by the pool. She was wearing a pink bikini. 'If you've bought me any of your stale rock cakes you can take them back to the forest.

I'm about to have a gourmet lunch. It will be delicious.'

Granny licked her long lips and smiled a toothy yellow grin. 'AND YOU ARE IT!' she snapped, grabbing her granddaughter with her newly polished nails.

The wolf must have bought a wish at wishit.com to trick Little Red Riding Hood so easily.

But before the girl was gobbled up, Mervin pointed his wand at the wolf and cried, 'All the better to zap you with!'

The wolf's head fell off to reveal Red Riding Hood's real grandmother.

'Granny!' cried her granddaughter. 'Thank goodness you're OK!'

'Watch out for the other grannies,' warned Granny Riding Hood. 'A gang of teenage wolves just burst in and gobbled the lot of them.'

Sure enough, when they turned around, a whole pack of fake grannies had surrounded them. The wolf-like grannies were licking their lips and getting closer and closer!

Mervin whipped out his wand and pointed it at the pack.

'Granny big and granny small,' he chanted,

   'We shall not be thy lunch at all,

   Throw off your wolfy, hairy fur,

   And be the grannies you once were.'

NOTHING HAPPENED!

Mervin's wand just drooped
in his hand like a wet lettuce
leaf. Araminta had wished for
it to stop working!

The hungry, snarling grannies closed in, stretching out their claws.

'Now hang on a second, ladies,' said Smartypants, thinking quickly. 'We're too

sweet to be your first course,
so why not start with a nice
meaty Crocodrag? I have one
with me.'

The grannies looked at each other and nodded.

'Better for our digestion,' they snarled. 'Crocodrag first and children, princesses and magicians for pudding.'

Smartypants whistled and Amazonia landed on the lawn by her side.

'Does it need pepper?' asked one of the grannies.

'No, it's hot enough already,' said Smartypants.

With that, Amazonia shot out a huge fiery burp that blew off all the fake grannies' clothes and singed their fur!

Princess Smartypants
and Mervin scrambled on to
Amazonia, and hitched Granny
Riding Hood up behind her
granddaughter.

Smartypants dug in her
heels and Amazonia whizzed
them up to safety above
the clouds. The Crocodrag
dropped Red Riding Hood
and her granny back home
before speeding off towards
Totaloonia.

CHAPTER 5

AN INGENIOUS DEVICE

As soon as they were back, Mervin hurried off to his laboratory with his soggy wand, hoping to find a spell to put it right.

Eric had been doing a good job looking after the castle and keeping an eye out for trouble. He'd heard lots of news about the crisis in Fairytale Land.

'It's a terrible mess,' he began. 'Hansel and Gretel made wishes for tons of gingerbread and sweets to build a house with but they scoffed the lot. Of course Araminta charged extra for

delivering the sweets so now
they're so fat they can hardly
move from the sofa. They just
watch TV or play interactive
games!

'Beauty wished for her
prince to turn
back into a
beast because
he was less
stupid
that way.

The trouble is, the Beast bit the postman and chased the grocery van up the road so no one will deliver letters or shopping to their castle. All, that is, except Araminta, who charges them twice the price!

'There's a cow going around the moon because the little dog thought it would be a laugh to buy a wish to see it.

'The Ice Maiden wished for a hot-water bottle and now she's melted.

'The hairiest monster in the forest bought a wish to be a character in a story book. His agent arranged everything and he is now so famous that he cannot get out of his new Mansion Cave for television and newspaper reporters!'

Eric was so exhausted by the endless list that he had to lie down for a while.

Meanwhile, Mervin was having trouble fixing his wand so he decided to use his computer skills to block any more orders for wishes getting through to wishit.com.

However, the Fairy Geek Mothers were ace Data Warriors.

'Ha ha ha,' giggled Harriet Hotkey. 'Some twit is trying to attack us with a Chewy Crocodile Virus. Let's send him an Explosive Rat. That'll blow his computer up.'

And that was exactly what it did. Mervin was furious.

'There's nothing else for
it. We can't go around fixing
wrong wishes all the time. We
need to stop this altogether.
We need to visit Araminta's
den and find out exactly how
she's doing all this without
being seen,' said Princess
Smartypants.

'Her house is never empty,'
said Doris. 'She leaves Calliper

there to guard it when she
goes out.'

Mervin took Princess
Smartypants and Doris into his
laboratory. He rummaged in
his cupboard until he found an
invention he'd built years ago.

'This is SPYBAT!' he
announced proudly, opening
a box. He pulled out a very
realistic-looking bat, attached
to a long piece of wire.

'There's a sound monitor and a video camera inside him. The signal is sent up the wire to these earmuffs and dark glasses. The glasses will show you what he's seeing, and you can hear sound through the earmuffs. All you have to do is lower him down Araminta's chimney. She's got hundreds of bats in her den so she won't notice another one. You'll be able to spy on her without her having a clue what's going on.'

'Brilliant!' said Princess Smartypants. 'Let's give it a go.'

CHAPTER 6

SPYBAT GETS TO WORK

Amazonia Sizzleflame landed on the roof of Araminta's cottage as gently as a snowflake.

Princess Smartypants and Doris put on the dark glasses and earmuffs and lowered Spybat down the chimney.

The result was incredible. The sound and vision were so amazingly clear, they could have been in the same room.

'We've done very well,' said Emily Encode. 'The government of Fairytale Land will pay anything for a wish to put its fairytales right again.'

'The price will be their
kingdom!' sniggered the little
witch. '"Araminta Allspell,
Queen of Fairytale Land." I like
the sound of that.'

'Cwark!' agreed Calliper.

'Once we have control of
Fairytale Land,' said Harriet
Hotkey, 'we can get rid of
that know-it-all Princess

Smartypants and take over her kingdom of Totaloonia.'

Up on the roof, Princess Smartypants went purple.

'So that's their wicked plan!' she fumed.

Down in the den, the Fairy Geek Mothers were showing Araminta how they were going to achieve this dastardly deed

with a nasty computer game
they'd made up.

'It's a combat survival
game,' said Emily Encode,
holding up her tablet. 'First
we get rid of that meddling
magician of hers.'

She pressed a key and
lighting bolts shot at a
cartoon picture of Mervin. He
disappeared with a pop.

'Then we attack her giant,
Eric. He'll try to defend the
Princess by throwing the
lightning bolts back at us. So
we'll chuck cyber-fleas at him!
He won't be able to fight back

because he'll be scratching himself bonkers.'

'Next we hit her squadron of Crocodrags with a virus which makes their scales and wings fall off,' added Gloria Gigabyte, showing everyone cartoons of Crocodrags looking bald and flightless.

'She'll have nothing left to fight with,' added Harriet Hotkey, and showed the next move on her tablet. 'Then we zap her with kissing beams so she turns into a frog and joins all those froggy princes she keeps in her moat!'

'Perfect!' exclaimed Araminta. 'I'm so pleased I bought your services along with my smartphone. You're delightfully horrific. We can't lose.'

Up on the roof, Smartypants gasped. Doris was so upset she slipped on a loose tile and would have fallen off if Princess Smartypants hadn't caught hold of her knicker elastic.

'What's that noise?' said Araminta suspiciously.

'Probably just a twig falling off the trees on to the tiles,'

said Gloria Gigabyte.

Araminta ordered Calliper
to fly up on to the roof for a
look. But before he had time to
hop as far as the windowsill,
Amazonia rescued the dangling
Doris and Smartypants. The
Crocodrag took off like a rocket

into the night sky with Spybat trailing along behind her.

Back she flew across the ocean to Totaloonia.

How peaceful it looked in the moonlight ... but Princess Smartypants was hopping mad!

CHAPTER 7

PRINCESS
SMARTYPANTS
MAKES A WISH

'How dare they!' shouted Smartypants, stamping her foot on the castle paving stones. 'The cheek of them! Trying to take over Fairytale Land AND Totaloonia! I should have banished Araminta Allspell after the time she caused trouble with the missing princes.'

'Why don't I just go over to Necromancy Nook and squash it with them all inside?' suggested Eric.

'They're far too clever for that,' replied Smartypants. 'I've seen what they're planning to do to us on that horrible computer game they're so proud of. No, we should turn the tables on them.'

'Those Geek Mothers are experts at digital games,' said Mervin. 'But until I find the right spell to get my wand working again I'm not much help. I wish there was some way of stopping them.'

'If only wishes were horses,' sighed Doris.

'THAT'S IT!' cried the princess. 'Wishes CAN be horses, and I've got my pony, Powderpuff, to prove it. We will win.'

Mervin and Eric shot each other a knowing glance.

Everyone knew Powderpuff was the worst-behaved pony in the world. She hated everybody except for Princess Smartypants and her quiet little pony friend, Misty.

'The Fairy Geek Mothers only know how to play computer games, so let's send them an invitation to come to the castle and play a real one,' said Smartypants. 'If they win they get Totaloonia, but if they lose they have to shut down the website, wishit.com, and never meddle with fairytales again.'

'I hope it
works,' said
Mervin. 'Um ... what
happens if you lose the
kingdom?'

But Princess Smartypants
was already at her desk
writing the invitation. She
whistled for the royal pigeon
and it flew off at great speed
to Araminta's, carrying
the envelope
in its beak.

The Geek Mothers shrieked with laughter when they opened the letter.

'She's playing into our hands,' laughed Gloria Gigabyte. 'Let's agree to go. She knows nothing about computer games. Totaloonia will be ours all the sooner.'

Araminta jumped up and down and clapped her hands.

'Accept her wish,' she cackled. 'WITH PLEASURE. Hee hee hee!'

The Geek Mothers were so used to typing that they didn't know how to do handwriting, so Araminta replied to the invitation for them. She handed it to the pigeon and he flew back to Totaloonia.

It was no surprise to Princess Smartypants that her wish had been granted.

CHAPTER 8

THE
GAME

On the day of THE GAME, everyone in Fairytale Land and Totaloonia came to the castle. Eric had been given the job of building the stands and had made them look like the ones at a medieval jousting match. The seats were packed, but there was a special area for the fairy godmothers at the front so they had a good view.

'If my wand was working I'd have conjured all this up for you,' grumbled Mervin.

'Thank you, Eric,' said Smartypants. 'It looks spectacular.'

The game was a gamble
because Princess Smartypants
would lose her whole kingdom
if she didn't win. Everyone was
on tenterhooks. (All except
Powderpuff, who was grazing
in her paddock with Misty,
dreaming up awful things she
could do to everyone except
her beloved princess.)

Everything was ready for the match between Smartypants and the Fairy Geek Mothers.

The Geek Mothers strode in at one end of the arena, looking slick in their silver and blue jumpsuits and metallic capes. They were armed with their tablets.

For a moment it looked as if Smartypants wasn't going to turn up.

'Your princess is too chicken to take us on!' shouted Emily Encode, waving her tablet at the audience.

The Fairy Geek Mothers were just about leave when Princess Smartypants arrived at the other end of the arena. She was riding Powderpuff and leading Misty, with Mervin and Doris on either side.

'Let's roll,' squeaked Gloria Gigabyte, pressing the start icon on her tablet. 'Where's

your machine and what
software are you using?'

'These are my machines,'
said Princes Smartypants,
pointing to her ponies.

The Fairy Geek Mothers
looked confused.

'I thought you'd recognise
the latest virtual computers,'

said Smartypants confidently. 'They can take any form you wish.

'The game we are going to play is called … Gymkhana,' she said, getting down from Powderpuff. 'Three people mount their virtual ponies and ride them as fast as they can in and out of the flagpoles. When they reach the end of the flags, the rider at the back slides off over the pony's tail, jumps into a sack and races through the poles back to the start. The first sack racer through the flags wins. If anyone falls off a pony they will be disqualified and their team will lose.'

The Fairy Geek Mothers laughed. It seemed such a stupidly easy game to them.

'You can have this pony. She's the fastest,' said Smartypants, showing them Powderpuff.

Then she jumped on to
Misty, and the pony knelt down
so that Mervin could hitch Doris
up and hop on behind her.

The Fairy Geek Mothers leapt
on to Powderpuff.

'Where's the start key?'
demanded Gloria Gigabyte.

'Just behind the saddle,' said Princess Smartypants. 'Give it a hard press.'

That's exactly what Gloria Gigabyte did.

Powderpuff was very angry that someone had prodded her in the back. She gave an enormous buck, sending the three Geek Mothers flying.

They hit the castle cobblestones with such force that they smashed into pieces!

There were clouds of smoke and electric flashes. Bits of wiring and circuits flew everywhere and the Geek

Mothers' heads rolled off into the flower beds!

THE FAIRY GEEK MOTHERS WERE ROBOTS. THEY WEREN'T REAL AT ALL!

This was an even better result than our princess had hoped for.

Princess Smartypants had known Powderpuff would buck because she always did if you prodded her. But she'd thought the grumpy pony would just chuck the girls off so they'd be disqualified from the game!

Everyone stood up to cheer, which almost muffled a terrible shriek from under the stands.

Araminta Allspell rushed out, sizzling with electric blue

sparks. Her hair had gone white
and was sticking straight up,
with her witch's hat resting
on the top. In her hand was a
melting phone.

'Heap of junk!' she cursed.
'I want my money back from
Witchphone Warehouse.'

The whole of Totaloonia and Fairytale Land roared with laughter.

Araminta shook her fist at them and fumbled in her pocket for her wand so she could turn everyone into something creepy and crawly. Then she remembered she'd left it at home, thinking that her smartphone had more power.

'Well, computer magic is a wonderful invention,' said Smartypants. 'WHEN it works.'

The crowd laughed even louder, especially the fairy

godmothers. They sang in unison:

'*Wave your wand and flap your wings,*

Chuck all computers in the bin,

Shake your bum, puff out your chest,

'*Cause our three wishes are the BEST.*'

Araminta got on to her broomstick and flew off in a huff towards Necromancy Nook with Calliper squawking behind her. At least she could count her treasure. That would make her feel better.

But when Araminta
arrived home to gloat over
her fortune, the room was
completely bare. Smartypants
had asked Doris to magic all
the fairyflonks away, and now
there was nothing left except
a very small mouse eating a
piece of cheese!

'That Princess
Smartypants
has done it
again!' screeched
Araminta Allspell.

EPILOGUE

Looking glorious in her new pink tutu and rainbow-coloured wings, Doris danced around the sky with her friends, showering everybody with glittering stars. The fairy godmothers were delighted to have their jobs back. When they began granting everyone three good wishes, Princess Smartypants was the first to ask for hers. She wished that …

1. All the bad wishes would be reversed …

2. Everyone would believe in magic (for if you don't, you will never find it) …

3. And everyone would live happily ever after.

Doris waved her new sparkly wand and granted all three wishes on the spot.

So Fairytale Land went back to normal and Totaloonia was safe from being taken over by Araminta and the Fairy Geek Mothers.

Mervin's wand had been instantly restored, too, so he decided to conjure up a magical feast to celebrate. It looked truly magnificent, laid out on jewel-covered tables in a beautiful Ali Baba tent.

Powderpuff and Misty were the guests of honour because they were the reason the Geek Mothers had exploded. Mervin magicked up some pony nut mix with extra apple slices for them.

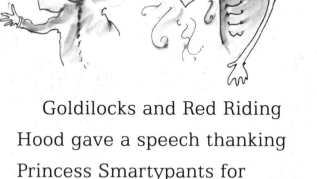

Goldilocks and Red Riding Hood gave a speech thanking Princess Smartypants for sorting out their fairytales.

Suddenly a wild roar of engines sounded from behind the castle gates. To everyone's surprise, a whole parade of grannies on motorbikes came speeding down the drive.

Princess Smartypants' first wish had turned the wolves at Elderly Gables back into grannies. Now they'd come to thank her.

VROOM VROOM

Smartypants climbed on to her own motorbike, Norton, and they all raced around the park. Everyone cheered madly.

Then the grannies joined in the feast and Mervin conjured them up some Arthritis Beer which they glugged down happily.

After dinner, Smartypants rode Powderpuff and led Misty back to their paddock on the other side of the wood. As they walked, she stroked her pony's neck, telling her how wonderful she was.

Suddenly the ponies stopped dead. Smartypants shot straight over Powderpuff's head and landed on the grass.

The ponies had been startled by a strange-looking white rabbit wearing a gold waistcoat and looking at his pocket watch.

'You're late!' he said.

'What for?' asked Princess
Smartypants.

The rabbit handed her a
letter.

'It's an invitation from the Queen to play croquet,' he said stuffily. 'Wonderland needs your help.'

'WONDERFUL!' cried Princess Smartypants.